我媽媽帶我去種菜

poetry & picture by maniniwei
translated by emily lu
my mom takes me down to the fields

我媽媽帶我去種菜,

在那個泥土房間裡。

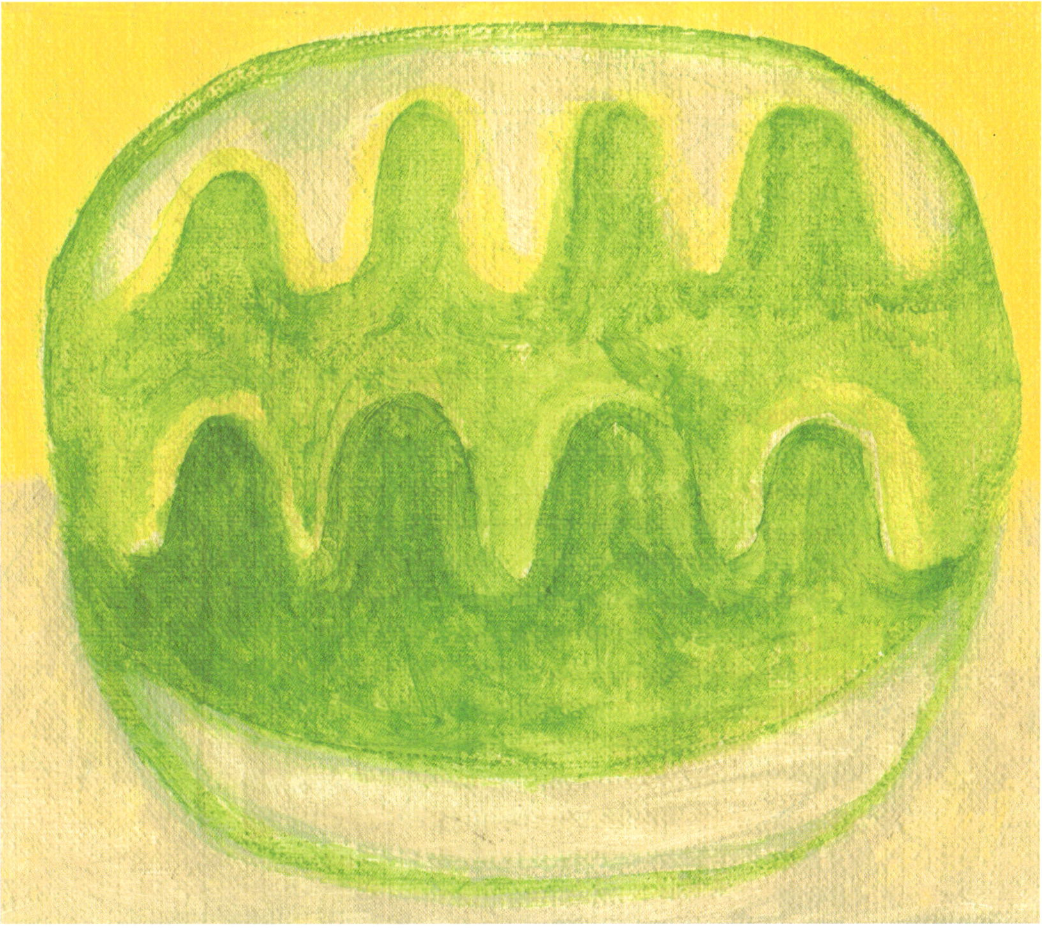

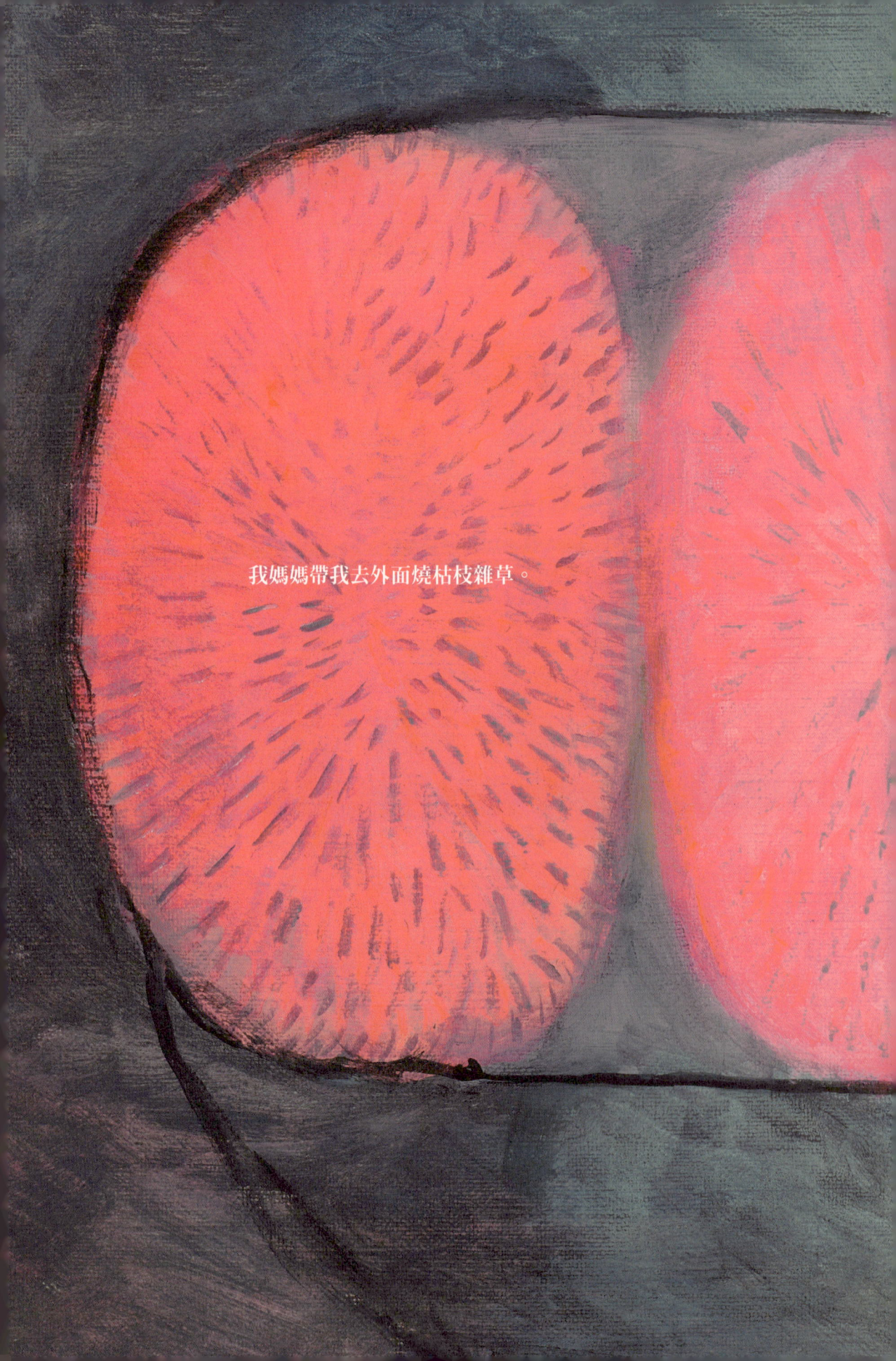

我媽媽帶我去外面燒枯枝雜草。

火很大，燒到我們都出汗了。

在這些我偷來的破爛上
在這些無法順利生長的東西上

我媽媽帶我去種菜

在那個泥土房間裡

我媽媽帶我去燒它

準備燒它

一點都不整齊

一點都不乾淨

燒到我們都出汗了

那些東西在那裡盛開旺開

盛開了像樹一樣繁殖

盛開了重新年輕

我一點一點的去燒它

去聞那些燒焦的味道

月亮已經剪掉那些人的壞舌頭

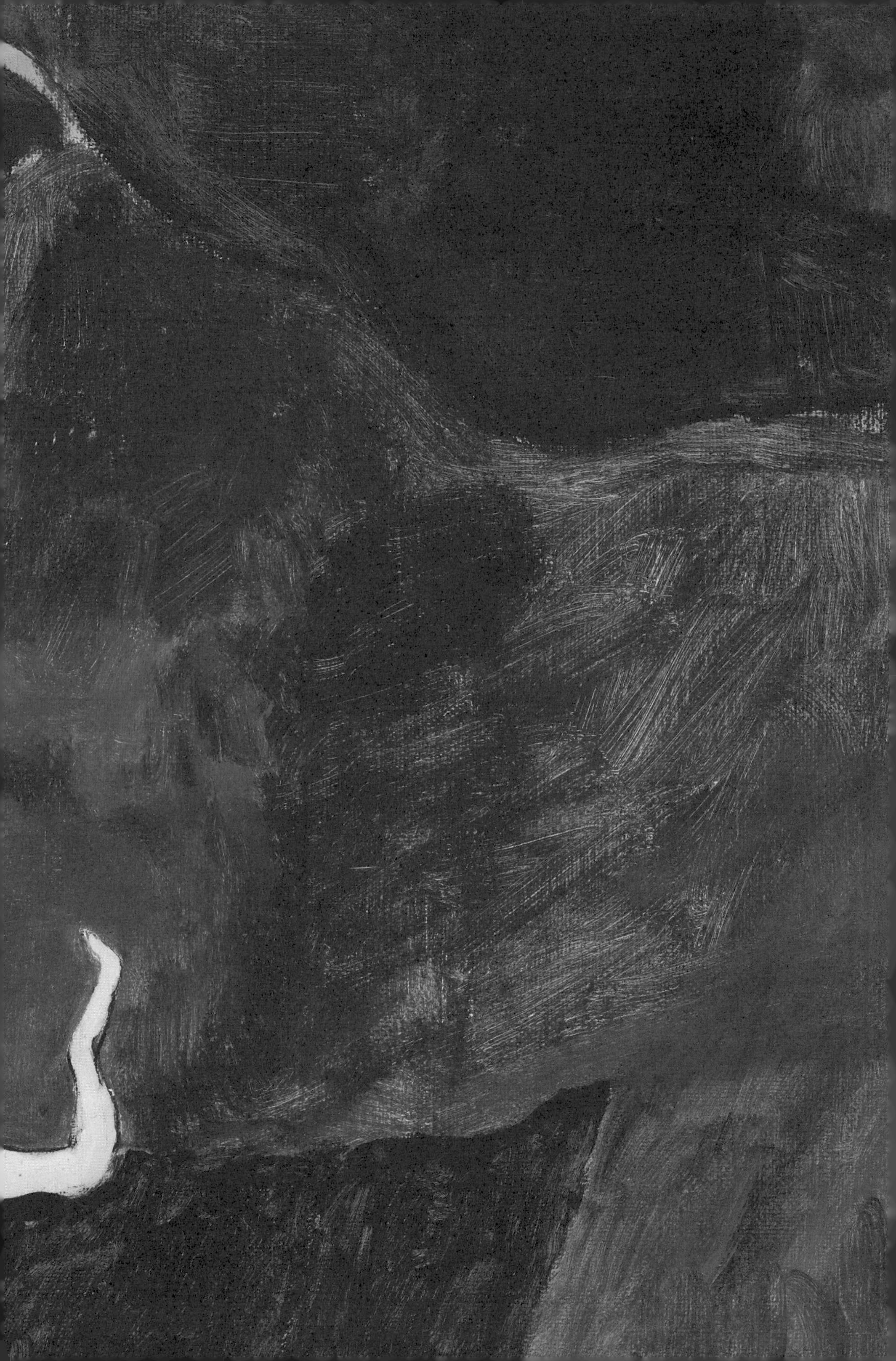

太陽已經砍掉那些人的壞頭腦

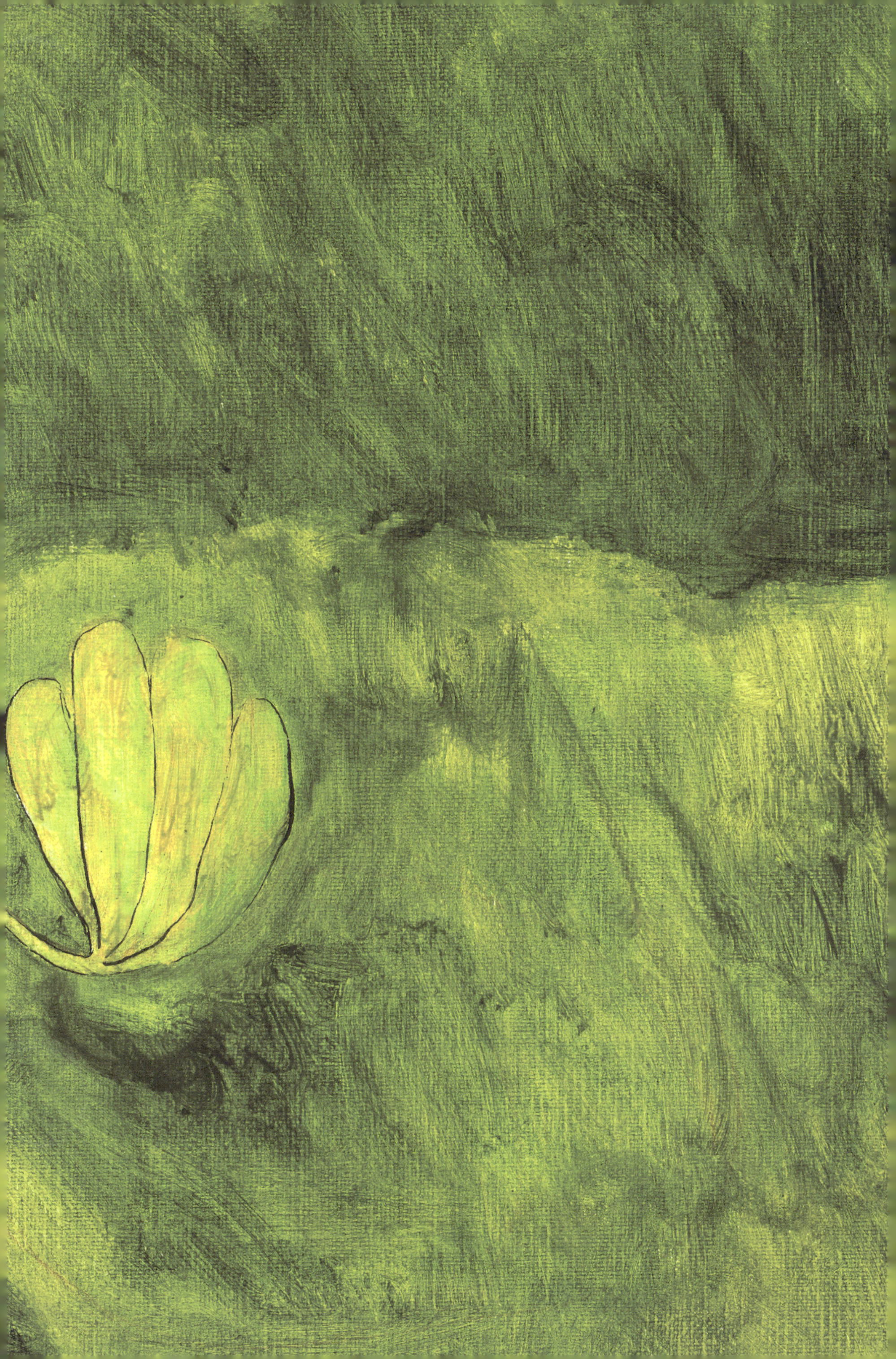

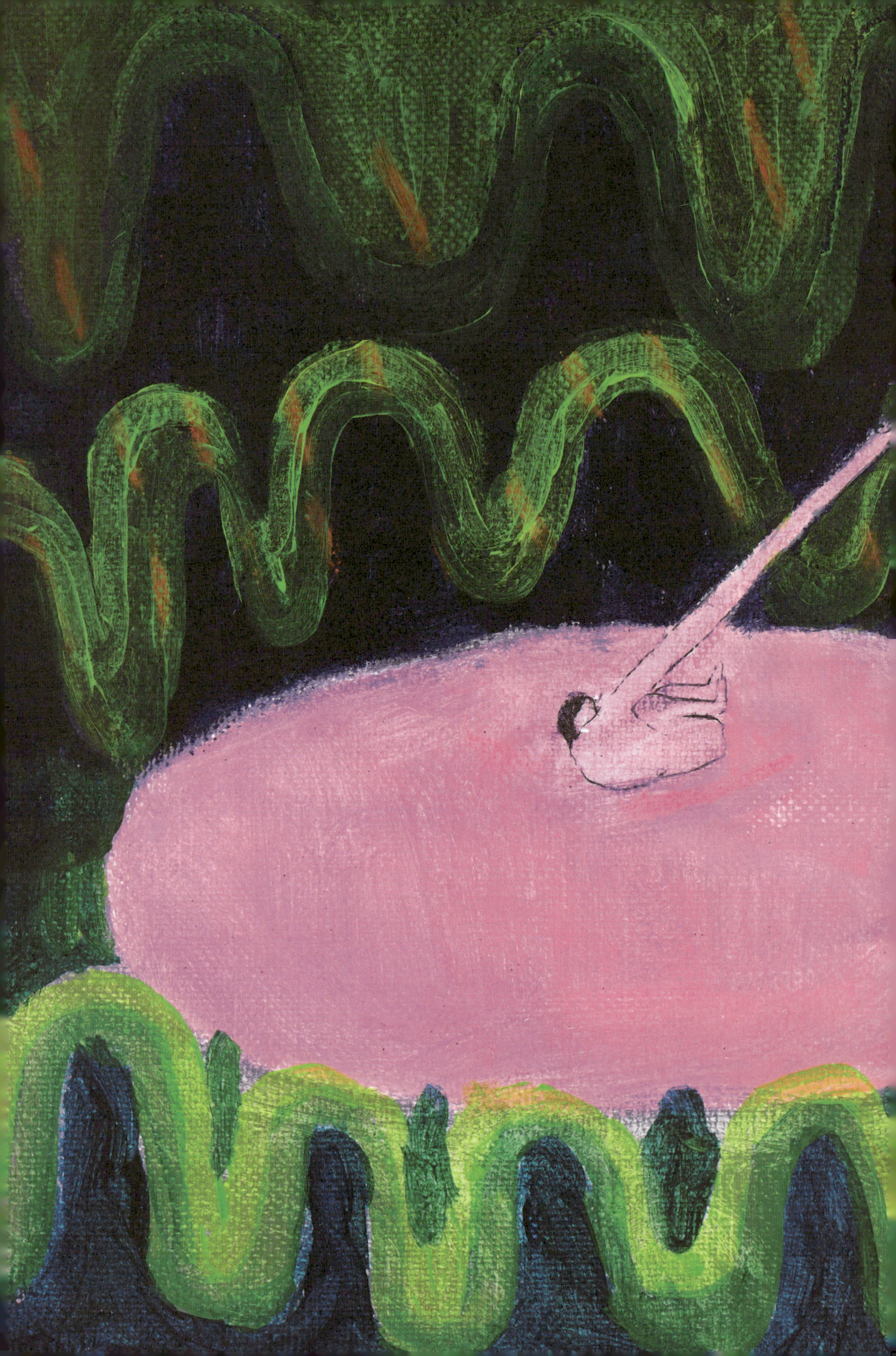

海水已經沖走那些人的壞身體

我媽媽帶我去燒它

我媽媽帶我去種菜

在那個泥土房間裡

火燒了時間

燒了一間又一間的房間

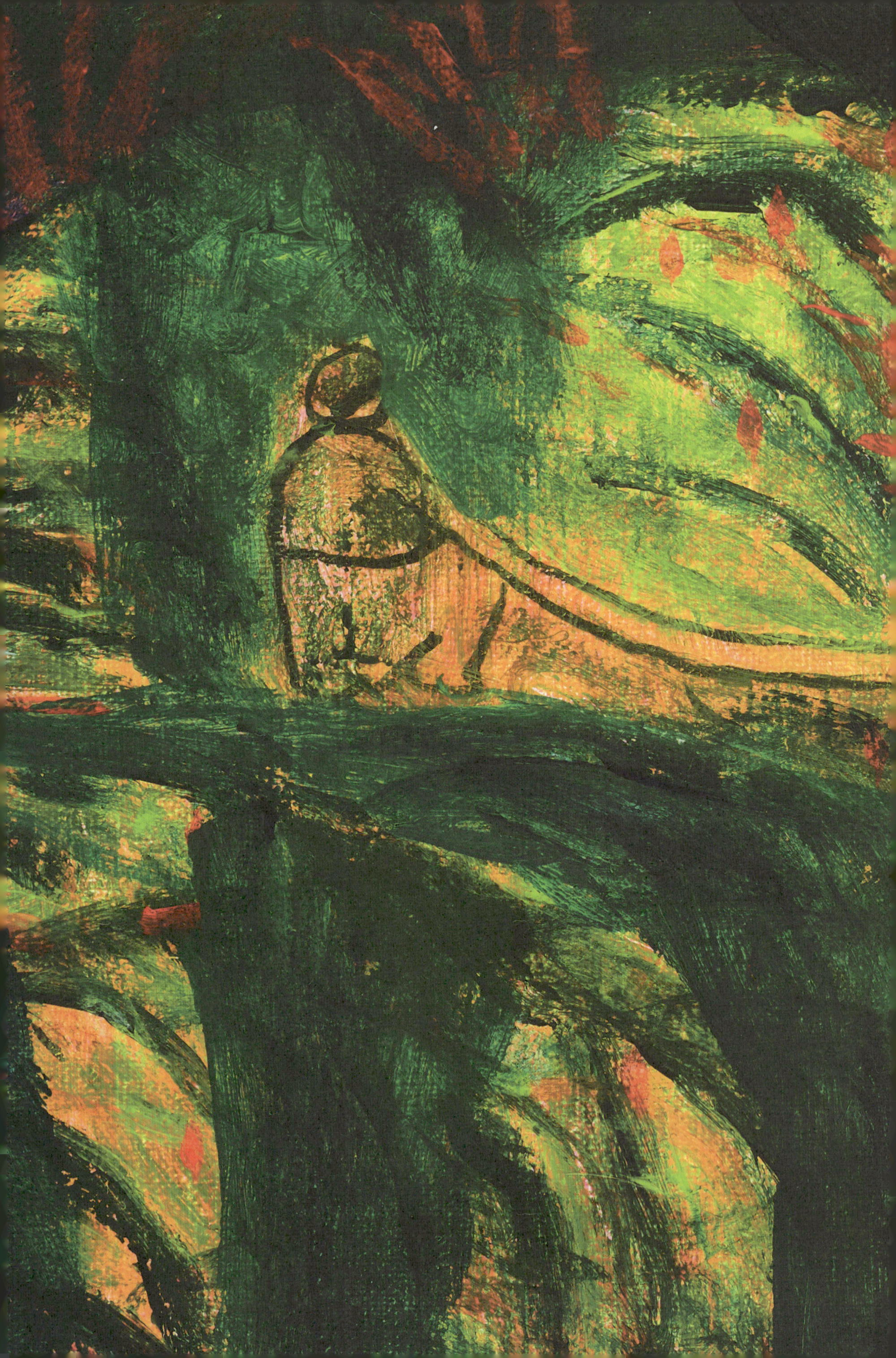

燕子醫生，我穿的是合適的破爛。這破爛得體、完整。

我需要的此生的泥土都有了。以前就有了。

我不可能對世界百依百順。火燒的土鐵硬的你不滿足的世界。

燕子醫生，那些事把我全身洗得很乾淨了。不管誰先死，先好好寫。

剛來了一條船。船身洗得很乾淨。

那種火燒的出汗。泥土的熱。髒溝水。我媽媽帶我去種菜。摸過那些。

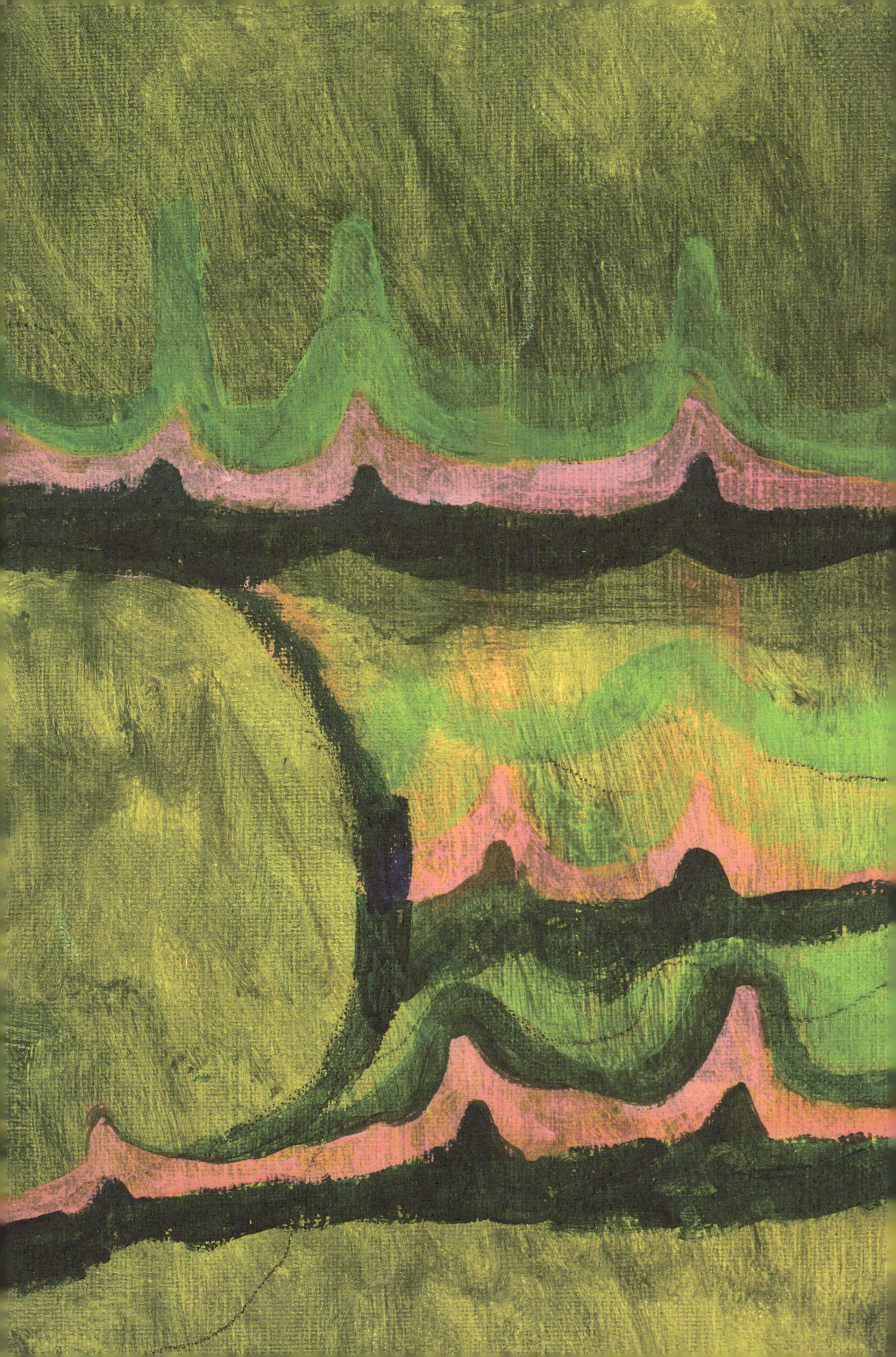

我媽媽帶我去種菜的路上被狗咬了。

我跟在後面。全部的傷她幫我受過了。

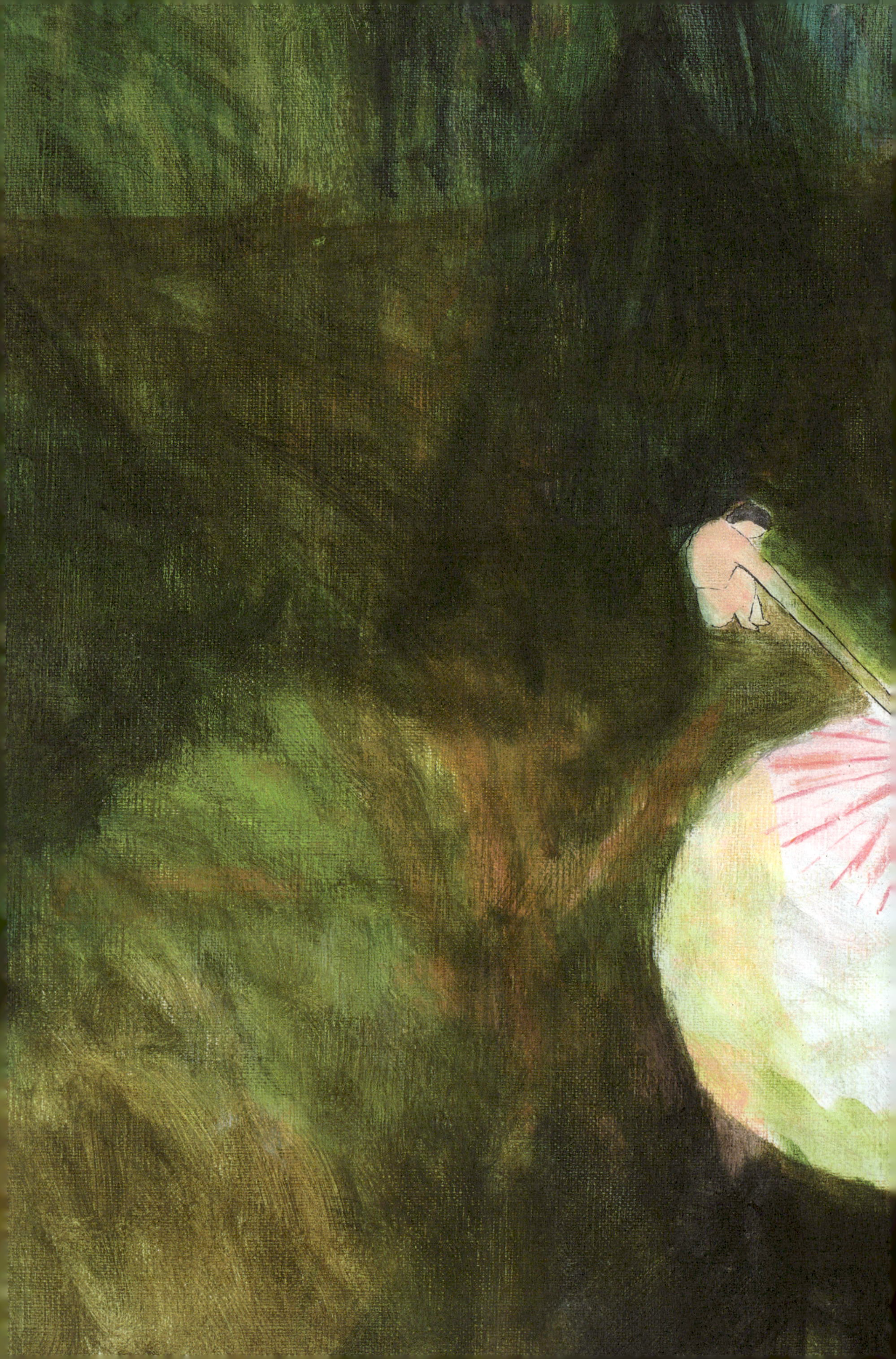

在黃昏的菜園裡,全部東西變得鬆鬆散散的。變暗的全部。最後要順其自然的。

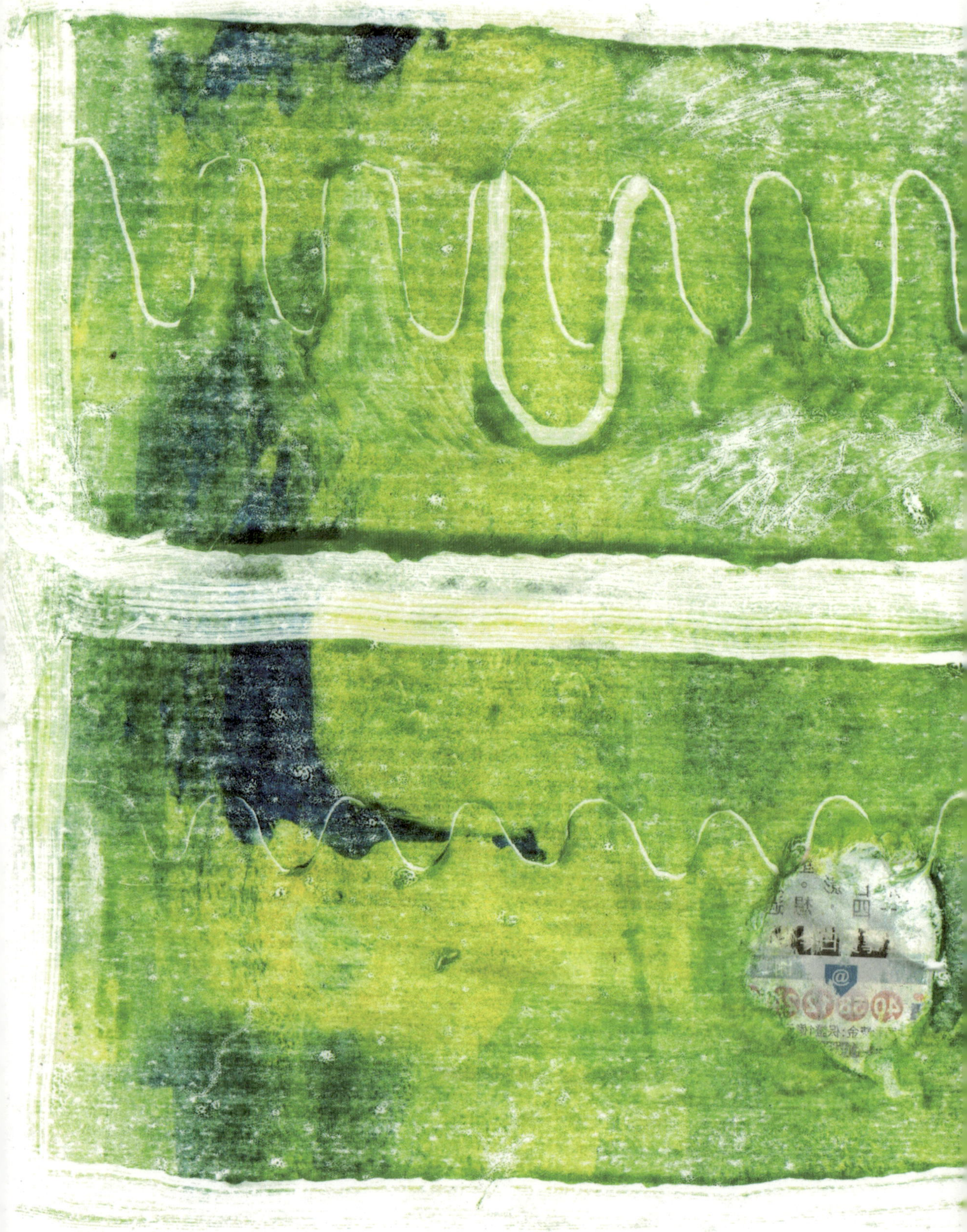

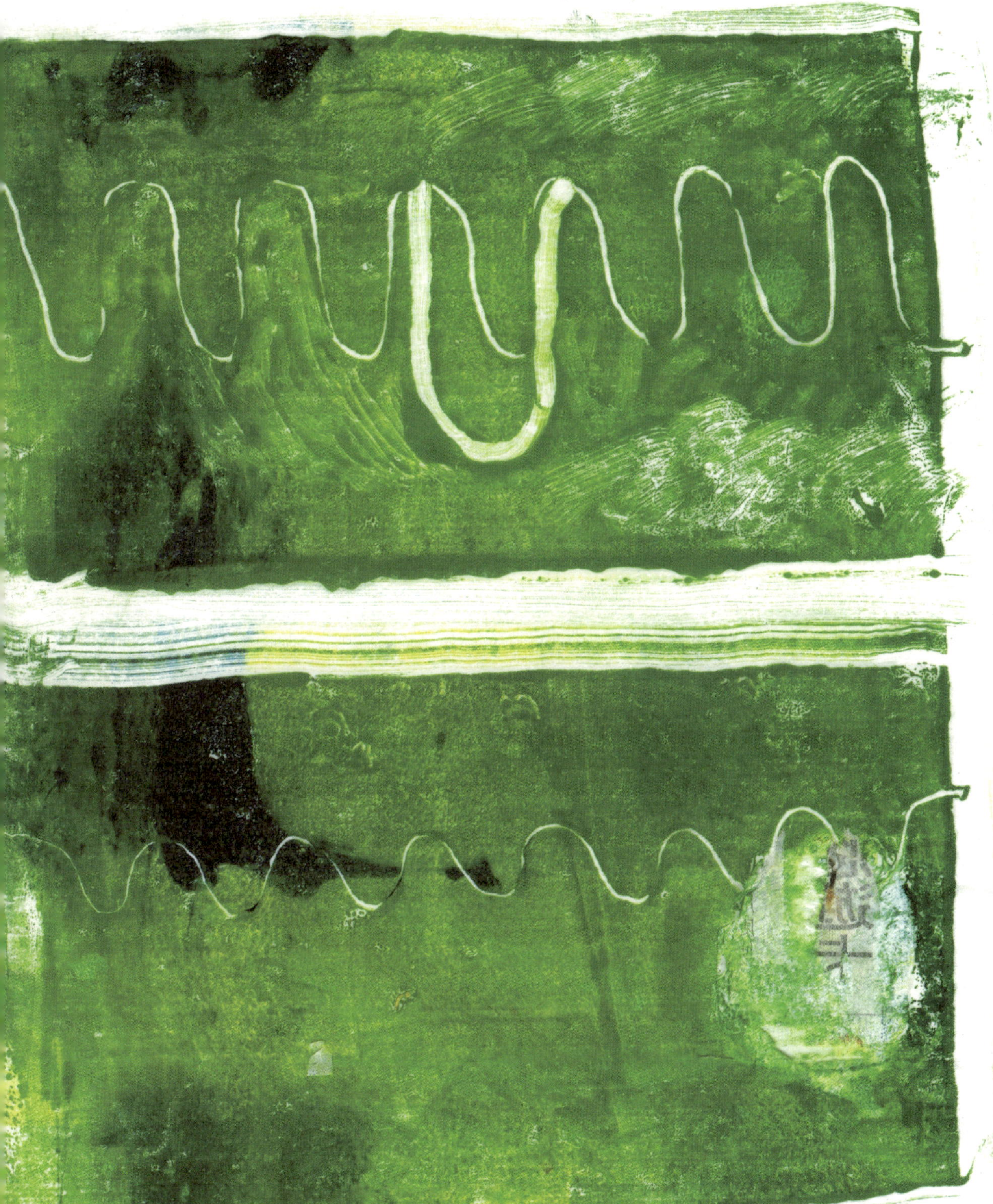

泥土房間

my mom takes me down to the fields

poetry & picture by maniniwei
translated by Emily Lu

my mom takes me down to the fields.
within that room of dirt.

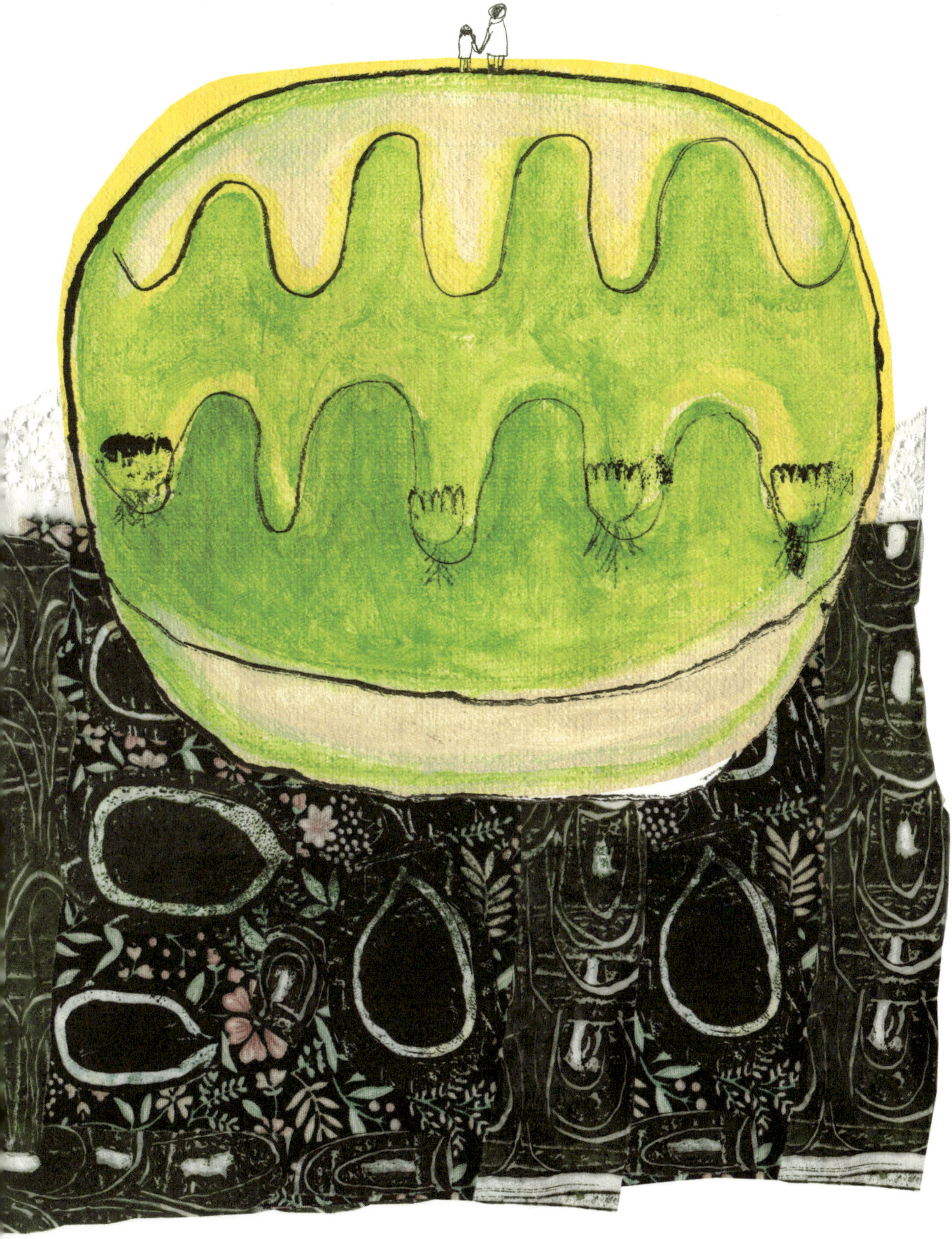

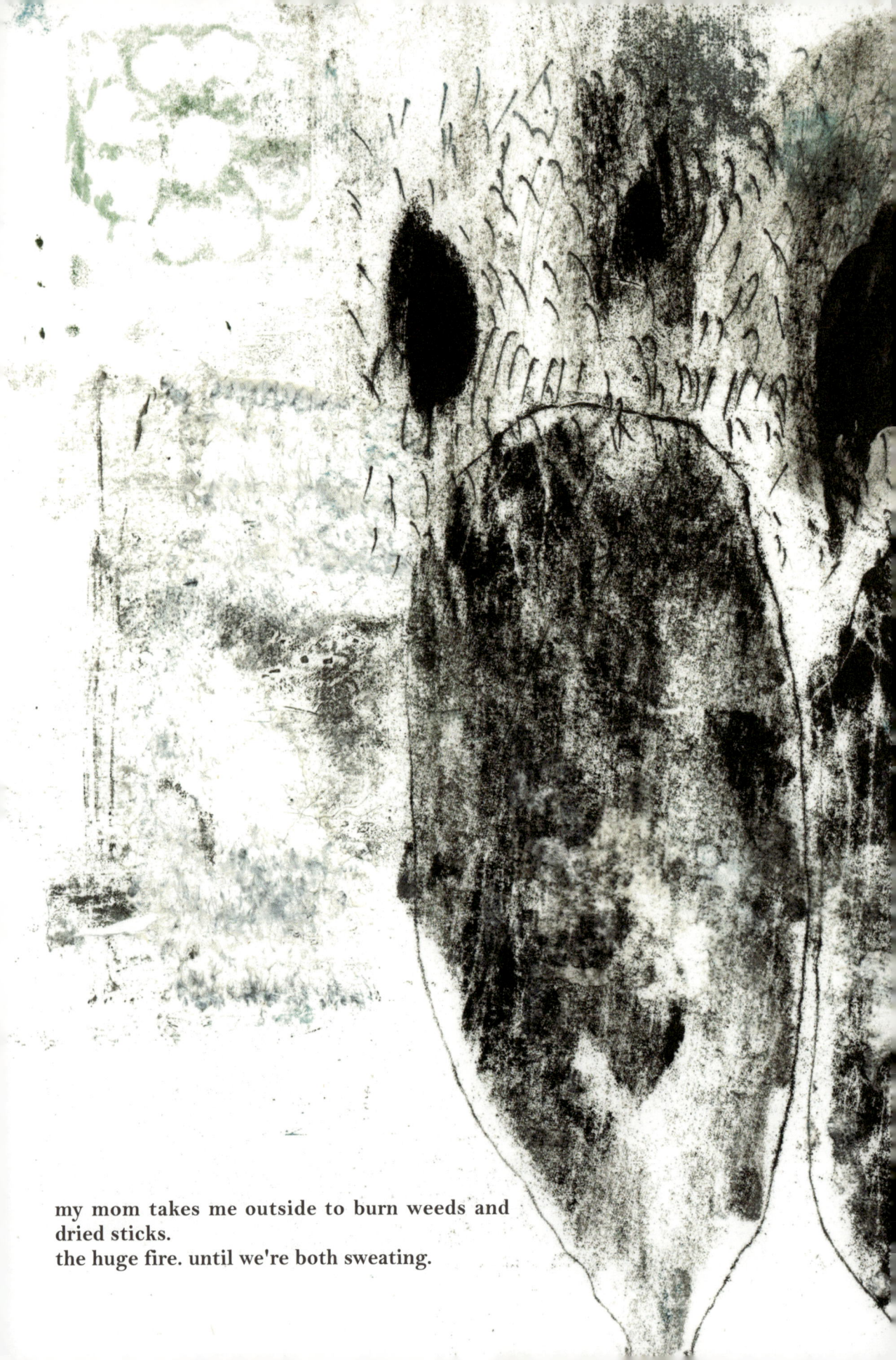

my mom takes me outside to burn weeds and dried sticks.
the huge fire. until we're both sweating.

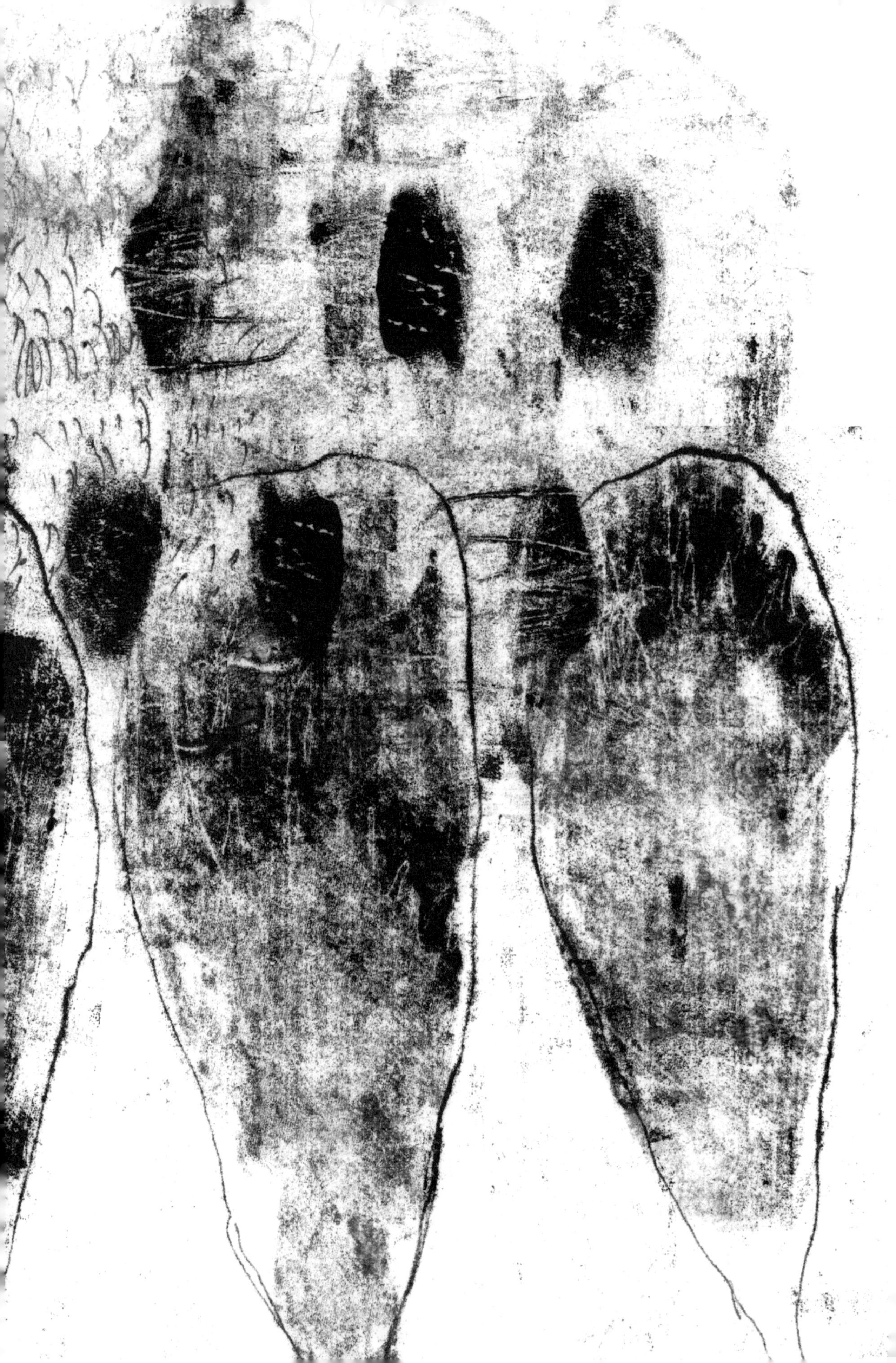

planting onto this pile of trash I stole
planting on top of what wouldn't grow anyway
my mom takes me down to the fields
within that room of dirt

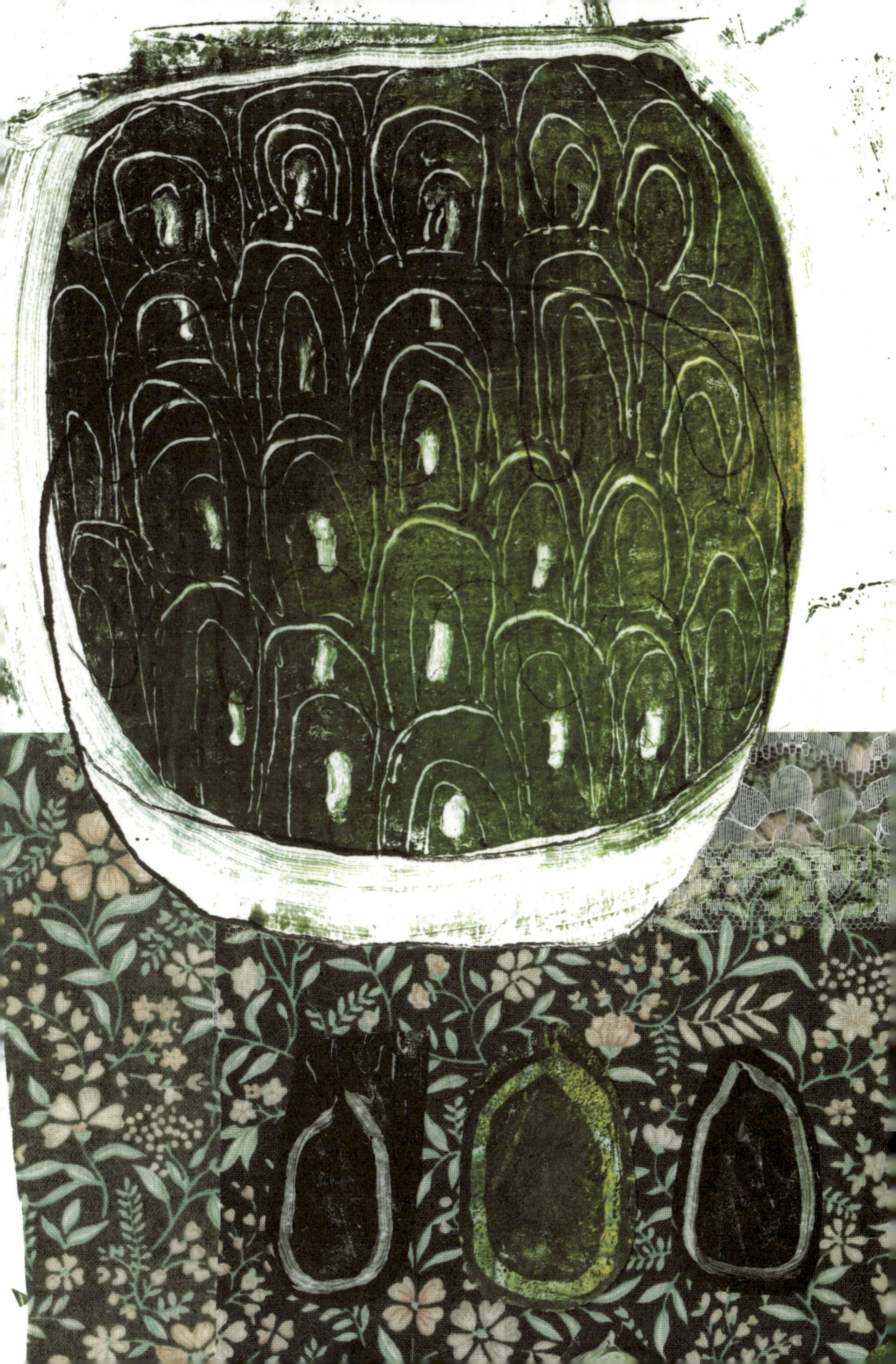

my mom takes me to burn it
to prepare to burn it
not neatly
not cleanly
until we're both sweating

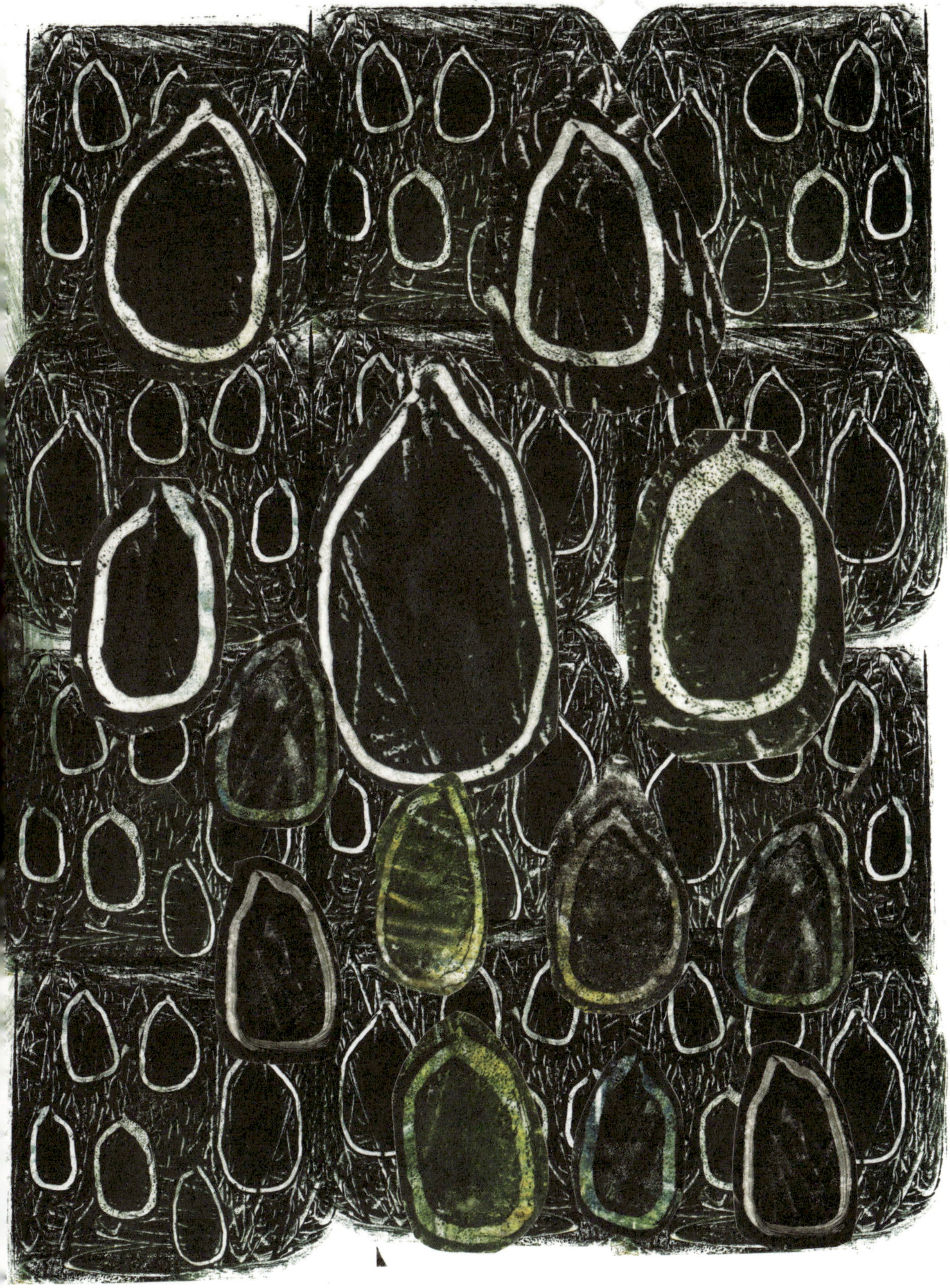

these things bloom deliriously
reproducing as trees do
there they bloom renewal

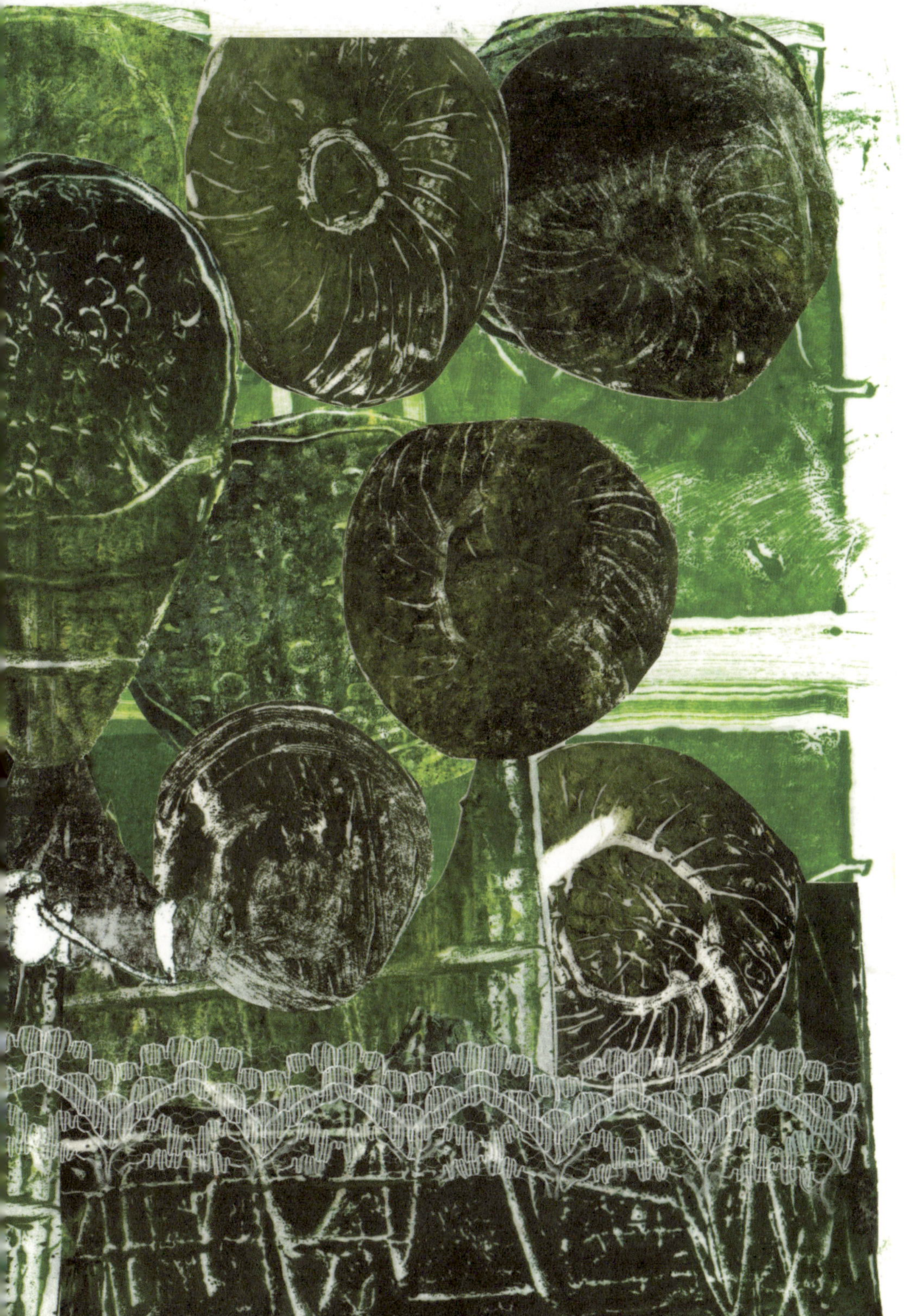

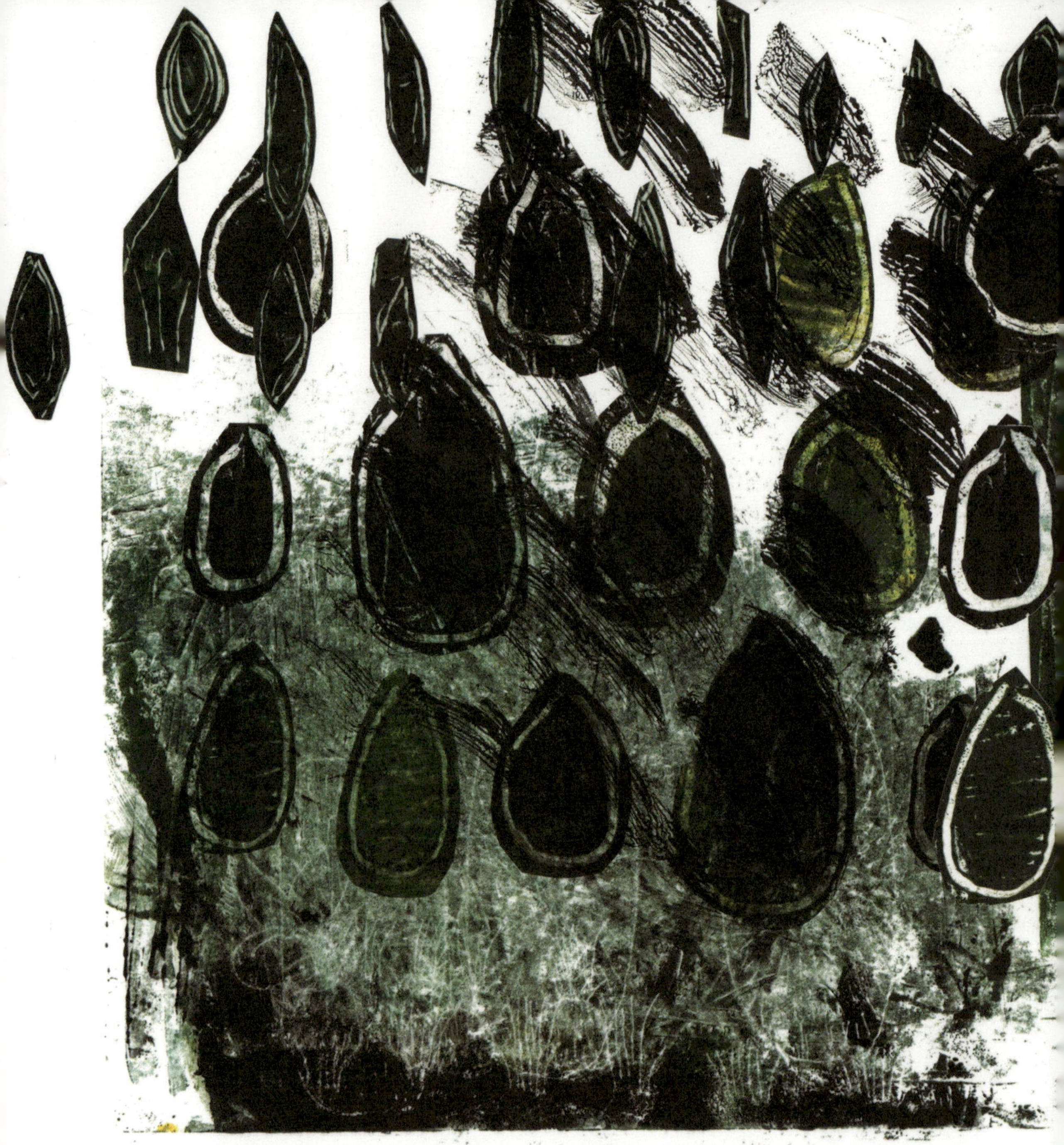

I go burn it bit by bit
I go breathe in that burnt smell

the moon has snipped off people's bad tongues

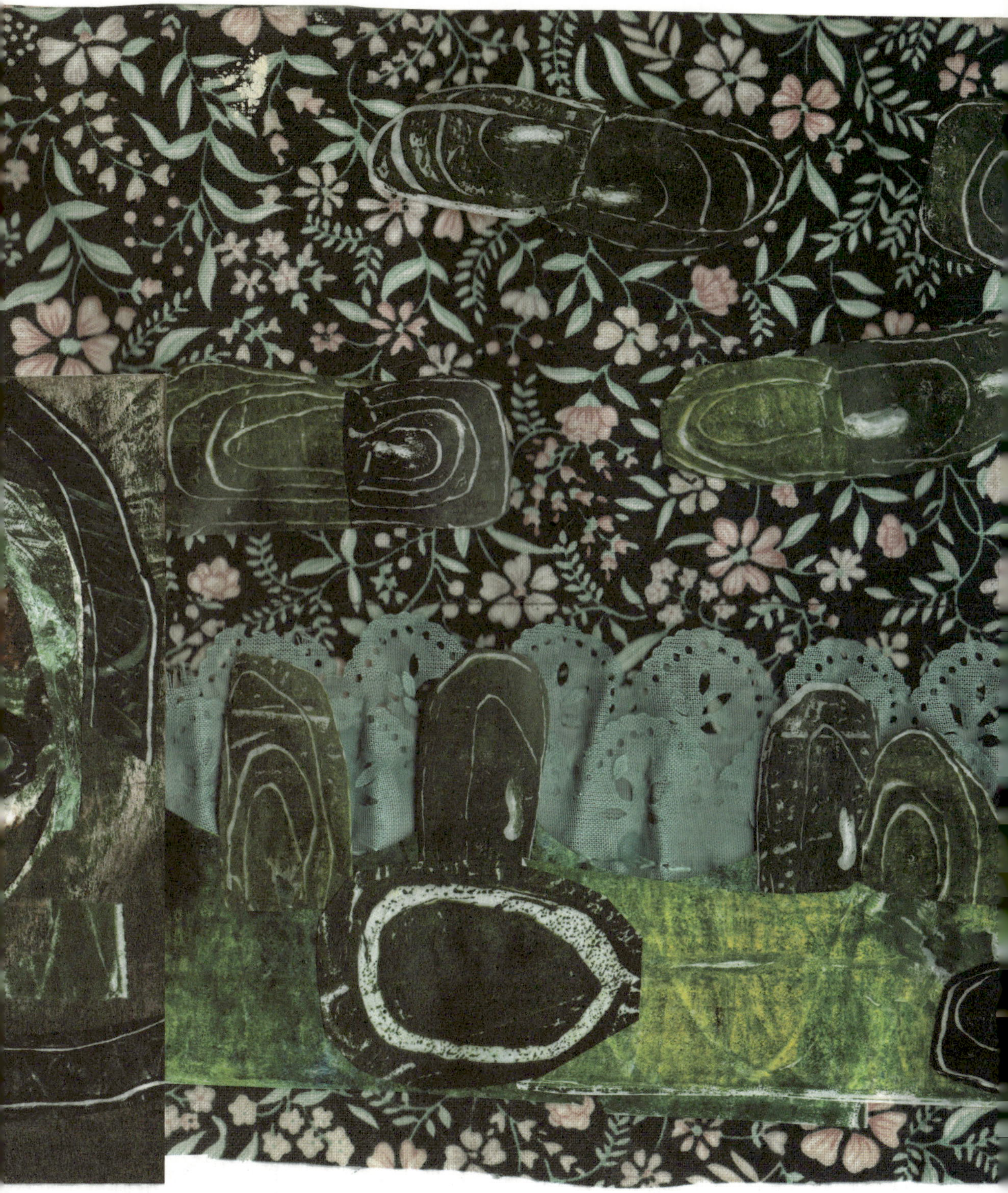

the sun has chopped off people's bad heads

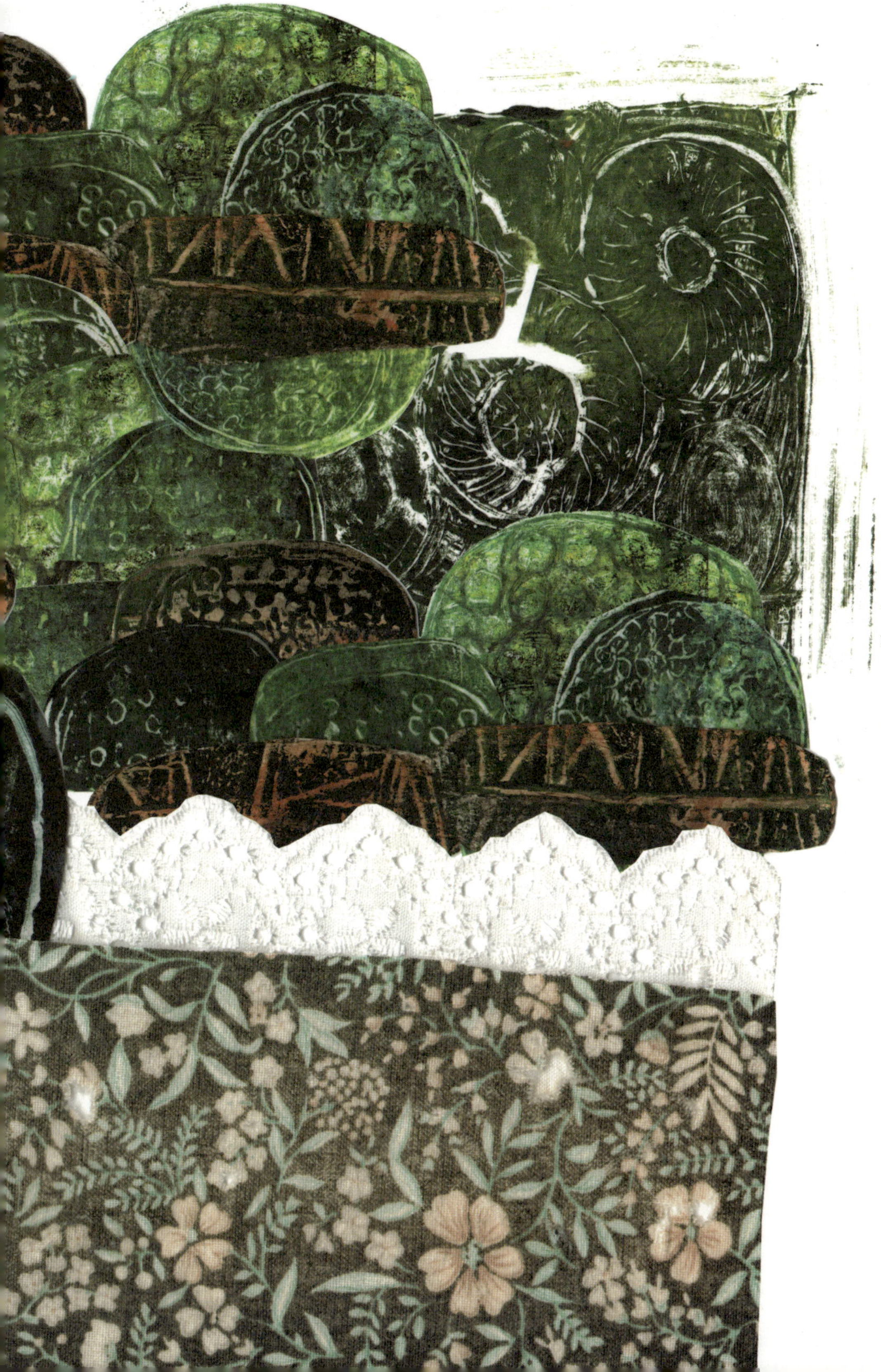

the sea has swept away people's bad bodies

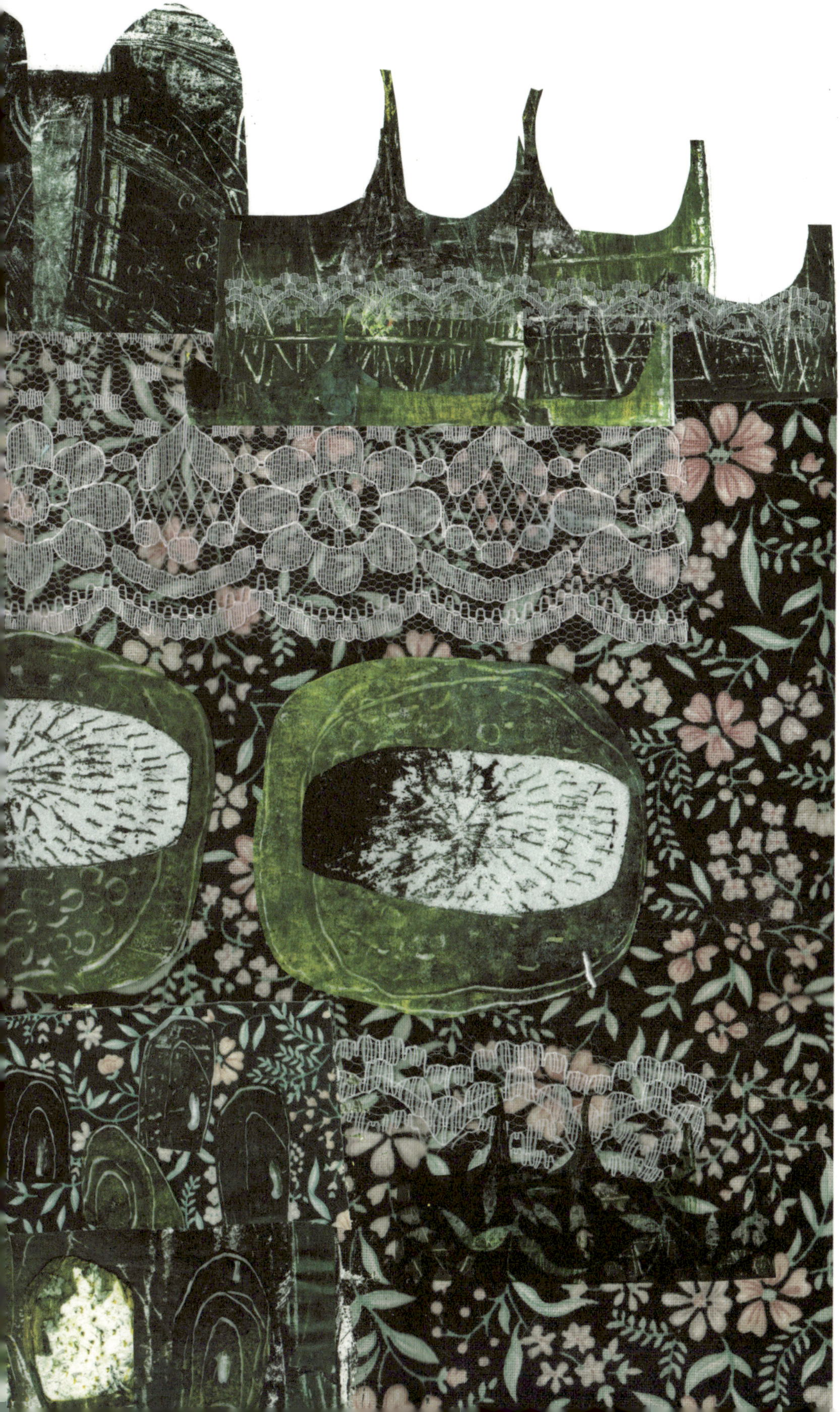

my mom takes me to burn it
my mom takes me down to the fields
within that room of dirt
time is burned away.
room after room.

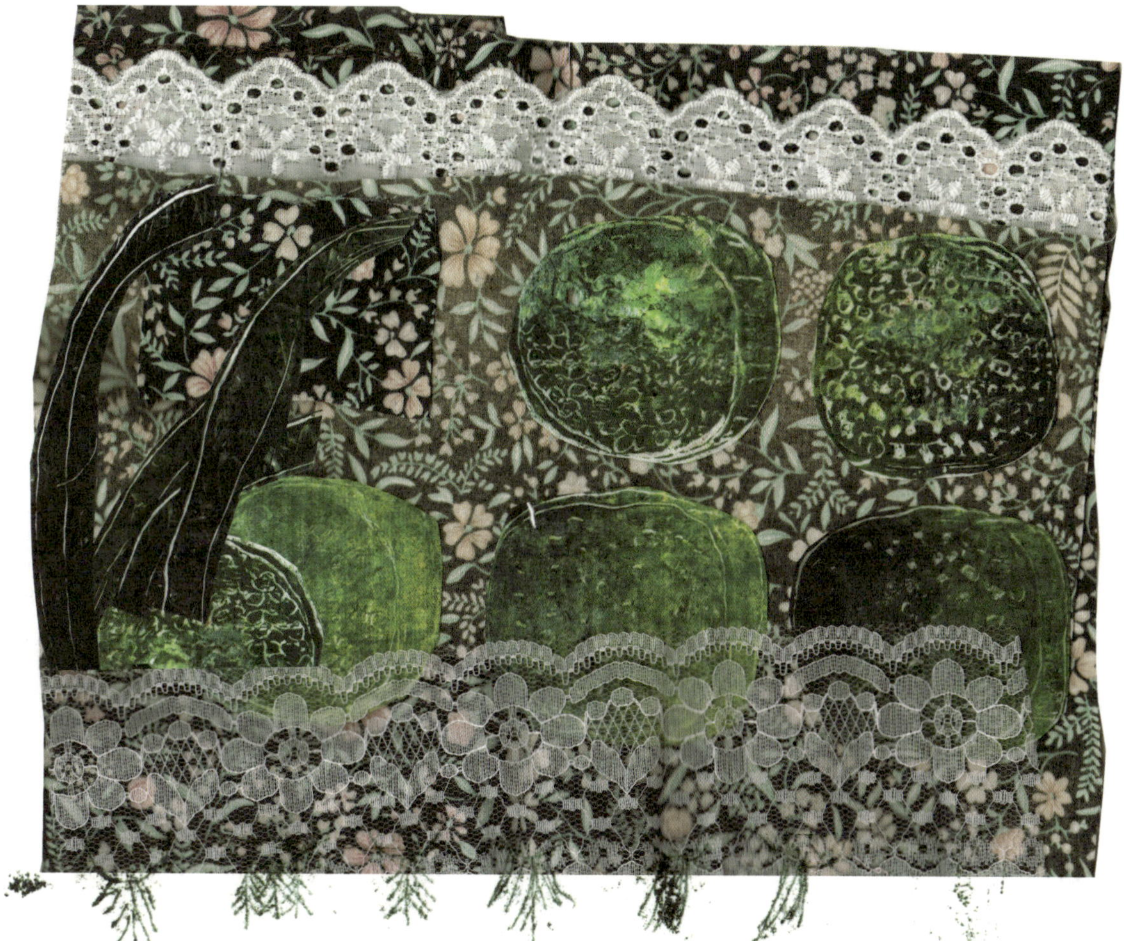

Dr. Swallow, I'm wearing scraps that suit me.
these scraps fit me wonderfully, completely.
I have all the dirt I need in this lifetime. I had it already.
I can't let the world do everything it wants to me.
scorched dirt hardens this world you find lacking.

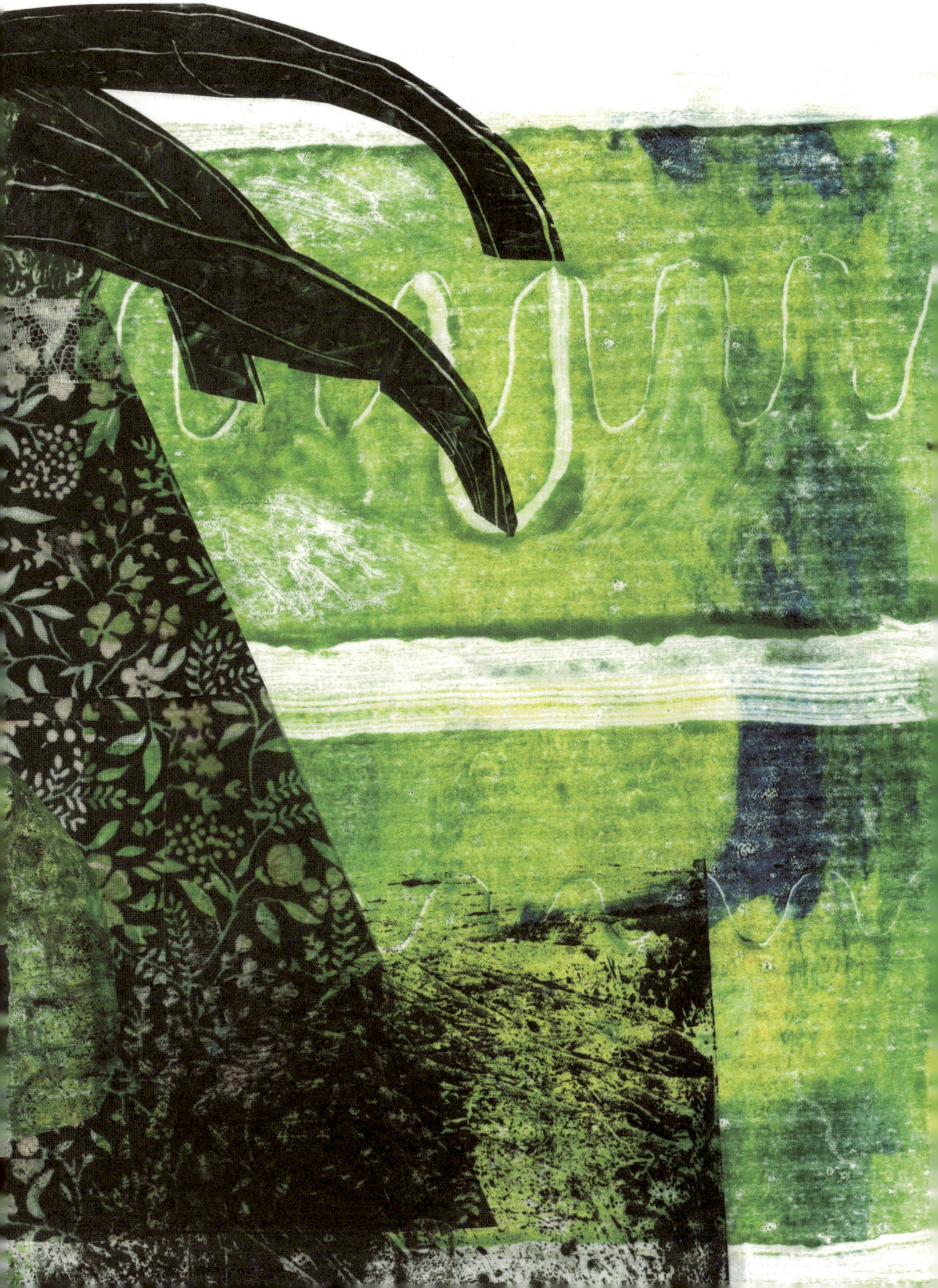

Dr. Swallow, those events scrubbed my whole body clean.
regardless of who dies earlier, first write well.
a boat arrived just now. its boat body scrubbed clean.

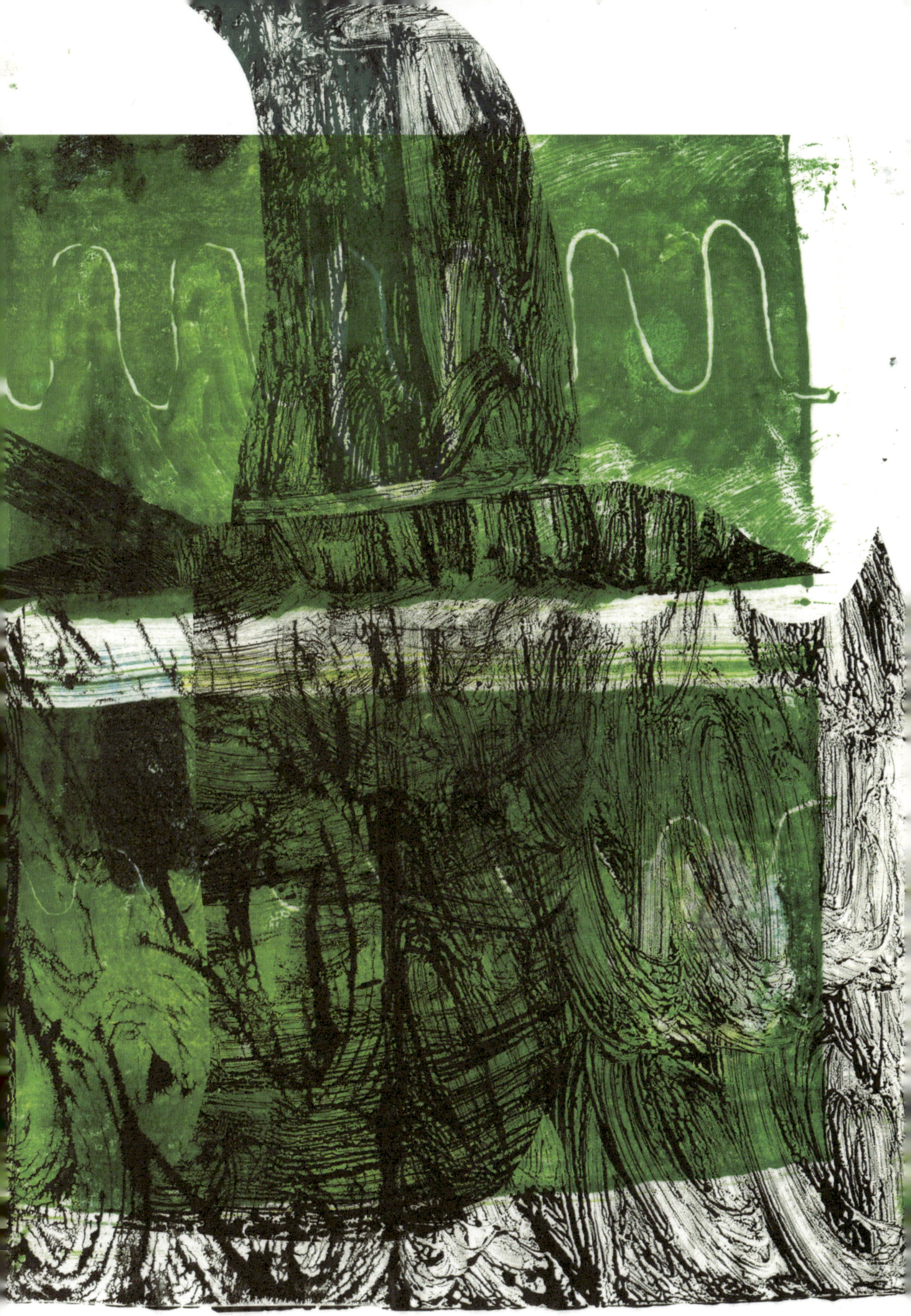

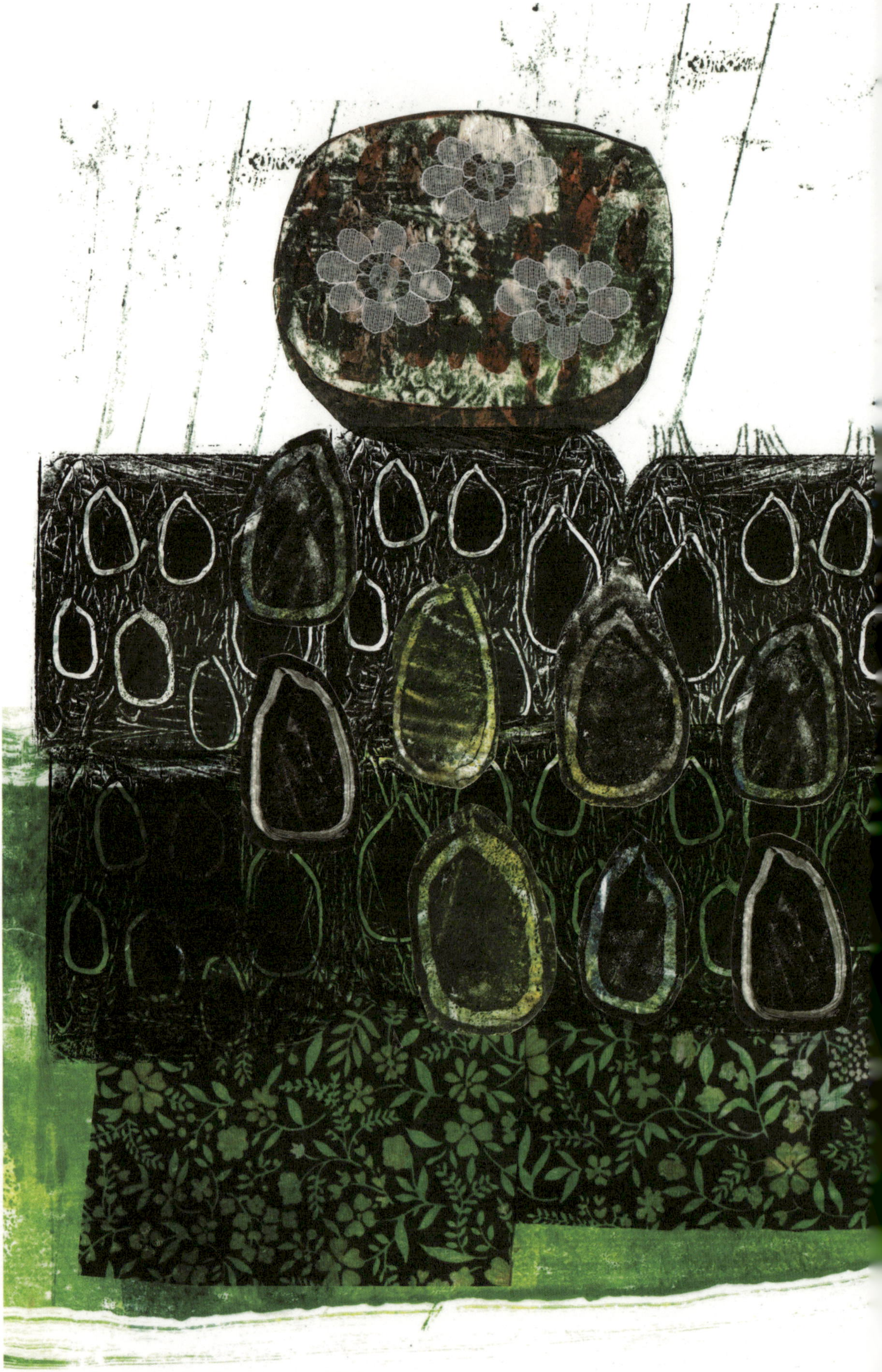

sweating over the fire. the heat of the dirt. the contaminated ditchwater. my mom takes me down to the fields. my hand over each.

my mom takes me down to the fields. on the way bitten by a dog.
I am following behind her. already she suffers in my place every injury.

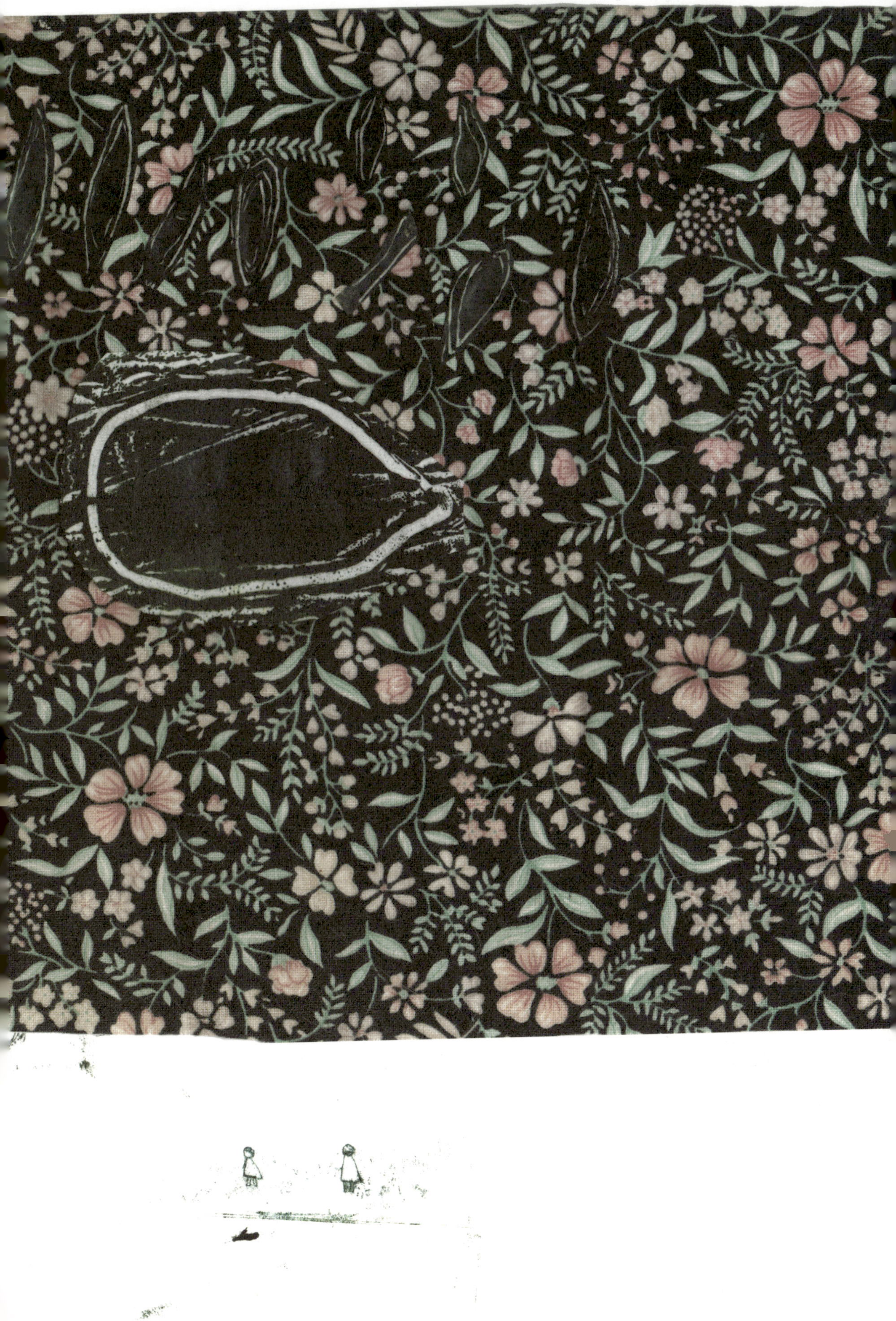

in the vegetable fields at dusk, everything has loosened.
the progression into dark. in its entirety. things tend to run their course.

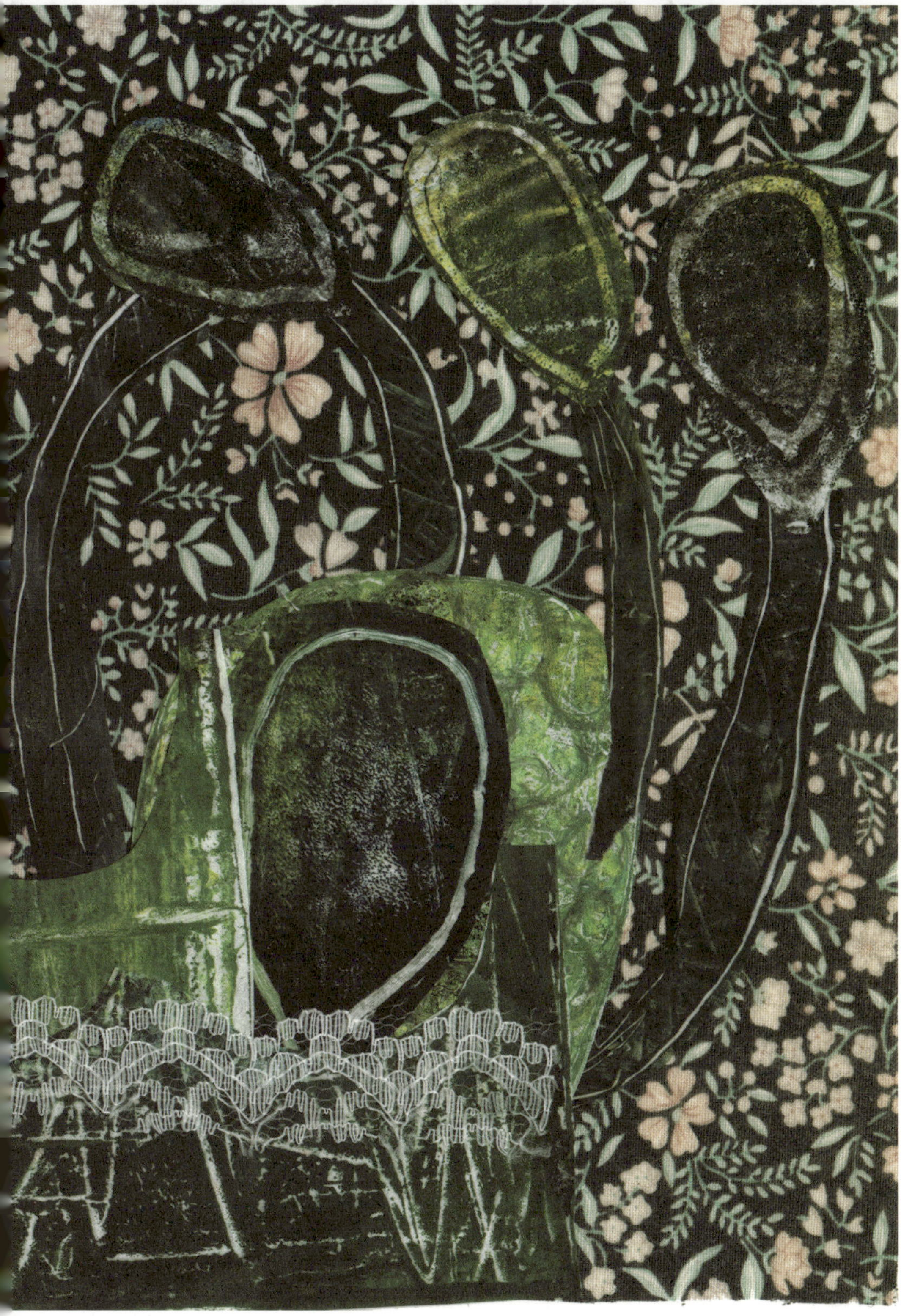

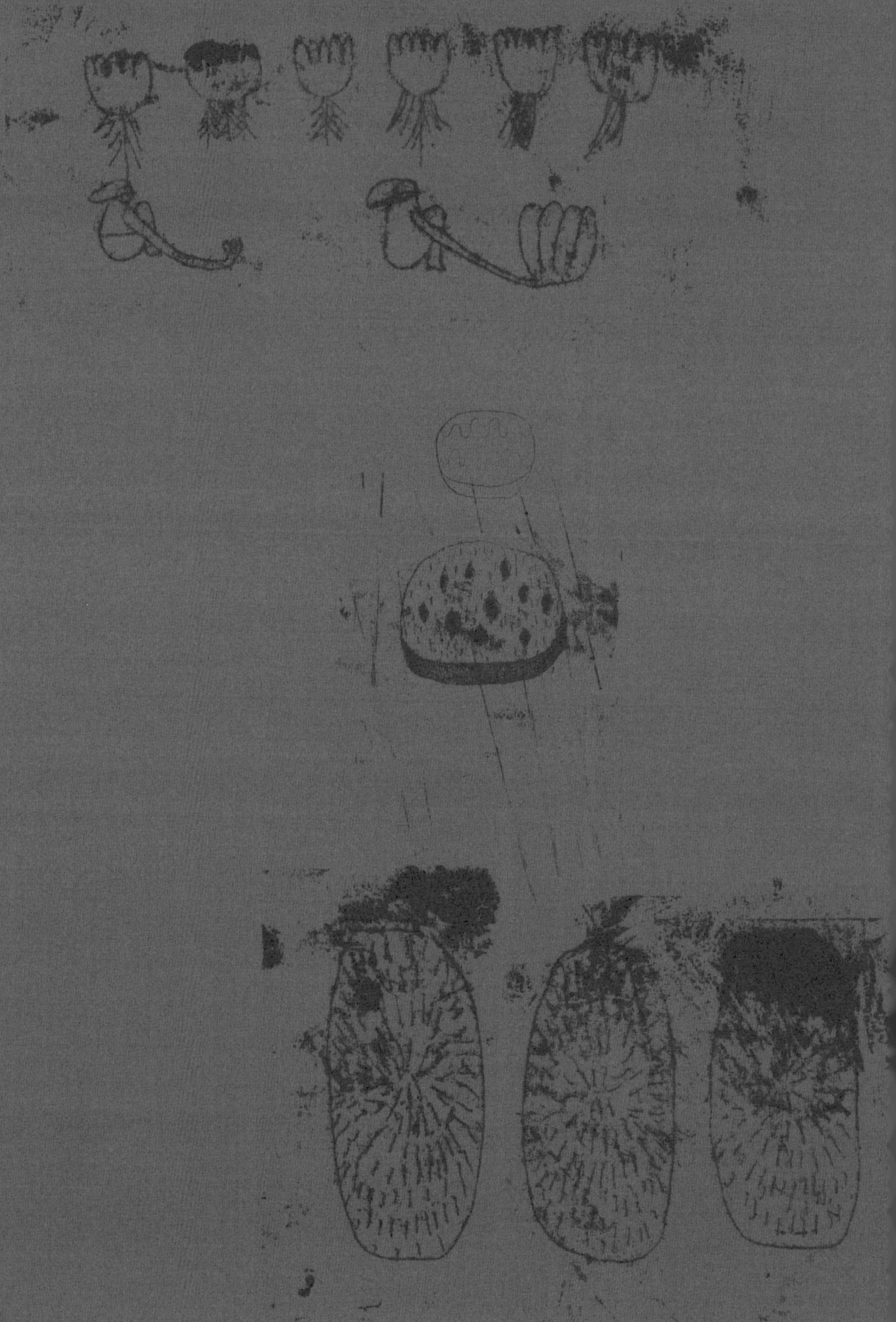

我媽媽帶我去種菜，
在那個泥土房間裡。
my mom takes me down to the fields.
within that room of dirt.

我媽媽帶我去外面燒枯枝雜草，火很大，燒到我們都出汗了。
my mom takes me outside to burn weeds and dried sticks.
the huge fire. until we're both sweating.

在這些我偷來的破爛上
在這些無法順利生長的東西上
我媽媽帶我去種菜
在那個泥土房間裡
planting onto this pile of trash I stole
planting on top of what wouldn't grow anyway
my mom takes me down to the fields
within that room of dirt

我媽媽帶我去燒它
準備燒它
一點都不整齊
一點都不乾淨
燒到我們都出汗了
my mom takes me to burn it
to prepare to burn it
not neatly
not cleanly
until we're both sweating

那些東西在那裡盛開旺開
盛開了像樹一樣繁殖
盛開了重新年輕
these things bloom deliriously
reproducing as trees do
there they bloom renewal

我一點一點的去燒它
去聞那些燒焦的味道
I go burn it bit by bit
I go breathe in that burnt smell

月亮已經剪掉那些人的壞舌頭
the moon has snipped off people's bad tongues
太陽已經砍掉那些人的壞頭腦
the sun has chopped off people's bad heads
海水已經沖走那些人的壞身體
the sea has swept away people's bad bodies

我媽媽帶我去燒它
我媽媽帶我去種菜
在那個泥土房間裡
火燒了時間。
燒了一間又一間的房間。
my mom takes me to burn it
my mom takes me down to the fields
within that room of dirt
time is burned away.
room after room.

燕子醫生，我穿的是合適的破爛。這破爛得體、完整。
我需要的此生的泥土都有了。以前就有了。
我不可能對世界百依百順。火燒的土鐵硬的你不滿足的世界。
Dr. Swallow, I'm wearing scraps that suit me. these scraps fit me wonderfully, completely.
I have all the dirt I need in this lifetime. I had it already.
I can't let the world do everything it wants to me.
scorched dirt hardens this world you find lacking.

燕子醫生，那些事把我全身洗得很乾淨了。不管誰先死，先好好寫。
剛來了一條船。船身洗得很乾淨。
Dr. Swallow, those events scrubbed my whole body clean. regardless of who dies earlier, first write well.
a boat arrived just now. its boat body scrubbed clean.

那種火燒的出汗。泥土的熱。髒溝水。我媽媽帶我去種菜。摸過那些。
sweating over the fire. the heat of the dirt. the contaminated ditchwater. my mom takes me down to the fields. my hand over each.

我媽媽帶我去種菜的路上被狗咬了。我跟在後面。全部的傷她幫我受過了。
my mom takes me down to the fields. on the way bitten by a dog. I am following behind her. already she suffers in my place every injury.

在黃昏的菜園裡，全部東西變得鬆鬆散散的。變暗的全部。最後要順其自然的。
in the vegetable fields at dusk, everything has loosened. the progression into dark. in its entirety. things tend to run their course.

IG/FB/website: maniniwei

詩、圖　馬尼尼為

馬來西亞華人，苟生臺北逾二十年。美術系所出身卻反感美術系，三十歲後重拾創作。作品包括散文、詩、繪本。著有：《多年後我憶起台北》、《我不是生來當母親的》、《我的美術系少年》、《馬惹尼》、《馬來鬼圖鑑》、《今生好好愛動物》、《以前巴冷刀.現在廢鐵爛》等二十餘冊。

英譯　陸悅洋 (Emily Lu)

詩人、譯者、精神科醫師。生於南京，目前定居多倫多。

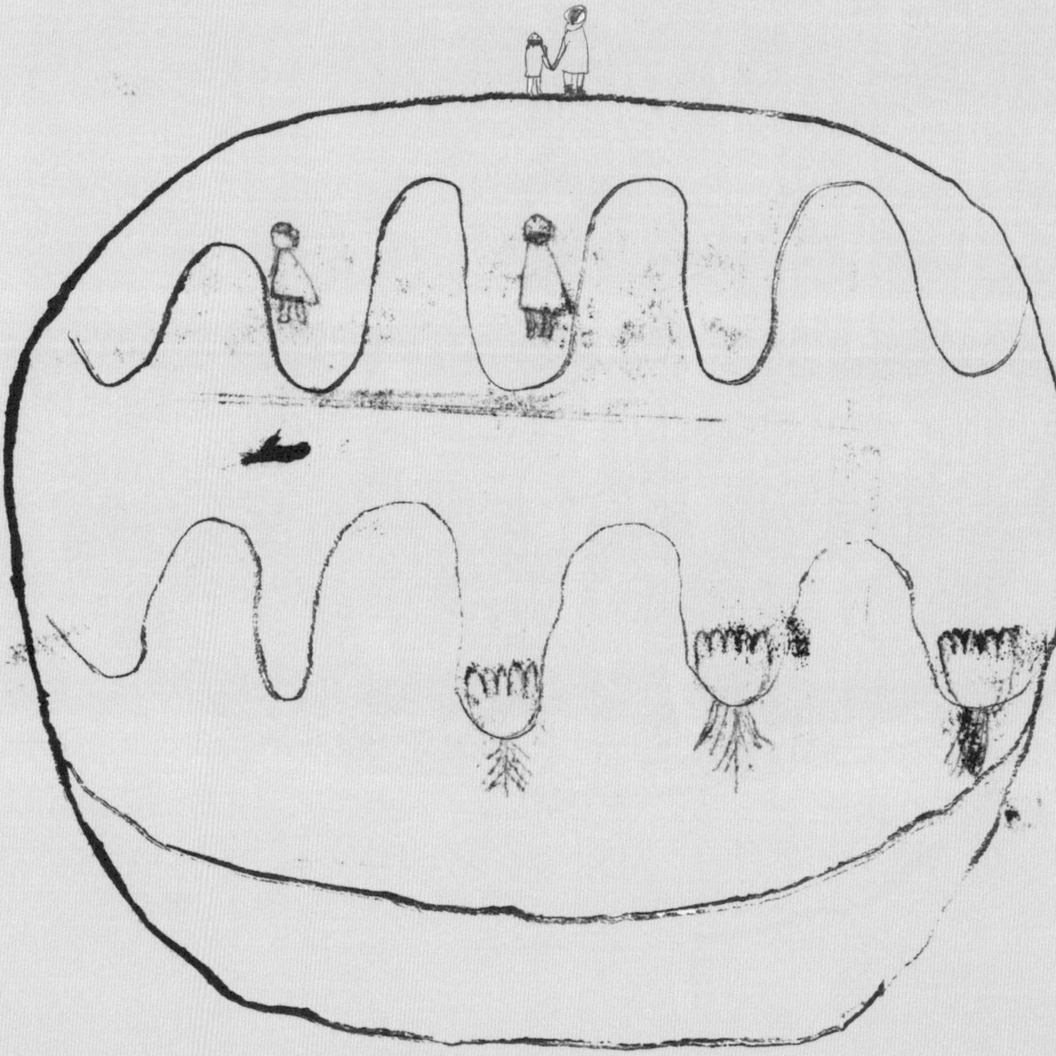

國家圖書館出版品預行編目（CIP）資料

我媽媽帶我去種菜 (my mom takes me down to the fields) / 馬尼尼為詩．圖．
-- 初版．-- 新北市：斑馬線出版社, 2025.05
面； 公分

ISBN 978-626-99484-6-8（平裝）

851.486　　　　　　　　　　　　　　114004381

我媽媽帶我去種菜
my mom takes me down to the fields

詩　／　圖：馬尼尼為 maniniwei
英　　　譯：陸悅洋 Emily Lu
總　編　輯：施榮華

發　行　人：張仰賢
社　　　長：許　赫
副　社　長：龍　青
總　　　監：王紅林
出　版　者：斑馬線文庫有限公司
法律顧問：林仟雯律師

斑馬線文庫
通訊地址：234 新北市永和區民光街 20 巷 7 號 1 樓
連絡電話：0922542983

製版印刷：龍虎電腦排版股份有限公司
出版日期：2025 年 5 月
ISBN：978-626-99484-6-8（平裝）
定　　價：500 元

版權所有，翻印必究
本書如有破損、缺頁、裝訂錯誤，請寄回更換。
本書封面採 FSC 認證用紙　本書印刷採環保油墨